BOB'S
FILM
FIASCO

A TEMPLAR BOOK

First published in 2013 by Templar Publishing,
an imprint of The Templar Company Limited,
Deepdene Lodge, Deepdene Avenue,
Dorking, Surrey, RH5 4AT, UK
www.templarco.co.uk

1 3 5 7 9 10 8 6 4 2

ISBN 978-1-84877-756-9

Designed by Will Steele
Edited by Libby Hamilton

Printed in the United Kingdom

BOB'S FILM FIASCO

SIMON BARTRAM

templar

IDENTITY CARD

Name: **Bob**

Occupation: **Man on the Moon**

Licence to Drive: **space rocket**

Planet of residence: **Earth**

Alien activity: **unaware**

WORLDWIDE ASTRONAUTS' ASSOCIATION

Chapter One

As he shot up into the air, Bob, the Man on the Moon, was worried. Never before in the history of the universe had he been summoned to Infinity House... on a Tuesday.

Yet, there he was, on a Tuesday, trembling in the lift, terrified. Infinity House was the headquarters for the entire cosmos and Tarantula Van Trumpet, Head of Moon Affairs, was waiting for him on the 17th floor.

"We must be in trouble," said Bob to Barry, his unusual dog and best-ever friend. "I hope Tarantula isn't cross about all of that nun trouble. They always go mad on their annual lunar trip.

I just can't control them!"

Bob had arrived armed with a special cake that he hoped would sweeten Tarantula's mood. It was spongy and creamy with the word 'SORRY' written on the top with jelly worms. Holding it high, and with Barry by his side, Bob entered Tarantula's office, bracing himself for a frosty reception. But once inside, he was most pleasantly surprised.

"SORRY?" enquired Tarantula, reading the worms on the cake. "There's nothing to be sorry for now. Please sit down. I have news."

Bob looked at Barry nervously as he took a seat. "So, Bob," began Tarantula, "do you like films? You know, movies, flicks, pictures!"

"Er, yes, Mr Van Trumpet," answered Bob, sitting forward in his seat. "Westerns are my favourites. Then spy films. Then comedies. NOT romantic comedies, mind you! I don't like all that kissing and stuff!"

"Of course, of course," agreed Tarantula. "And tell me, are you familiar with the actor, Frankie Las Vegas?"

"FRANKIE LAS VEGAS!" exclaimed Bob. "Oh yes!!! Just last week I watched him in *GHOST COP 6*. He played this phantom policeman who carried his head under his arm and solved crimes from beyond the grave!"

"Sounds erm… interesting," said Tarantula.

"Oh, it was, sir. There was this master villain called Professor Monocle and he sucked up Frankie's ghostly head with a mini-vacuum cleaner."

"Really?"

"Yes. It was a bit too realistic, to tell you the truth. I got a little worried. I was actually pretty relieved to see Frankie the following night on a chat show. Thankfully his head was back on all right!"

"Well he'll certainly need it for his next big role," said Tarantula. "Otherwise where on earth would he put his helmet?"

"His helmet?" beamed Bob. "What character is he going to play? A fireman? Or a rally driver? Oh, NO, NO, I've got it… A ROMAN SOLDIER!"

"No, Bob, he isn't going to be any of those," answered Tarantula, the sunlight dancing upon his spectacles. "He's going to be… THE MAN ON THE MOON!"

Bob's eyes widened.

"THE MAN ON THE MOON!?" he cried in amazement.

"Yes, Bob," confirmed Tarantula. "He's going to be YOU!"

Bob almost fainted in his chair.

"M-M-ME?" he said.

"Yes, you," smiled Tarantula. "Tell me, Bob, do you remember Tommy Potato's cat?"

"Er… yes," answered Bob. "It jumped down into Crater 306 after chasing Tommy's remote-control lunar buggy. I rescued it using two pilchards, some glue rope and a moon boot."

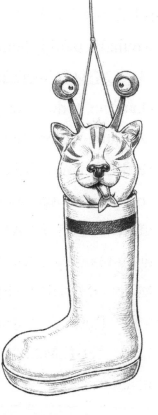

"That's right," said Tarantula, "and let me tell you, the world remembers too. That rescue was captured on a mobile phone and now it's a huge MoonTube sensation!"

"Gosh!" gasped Bob, as Tarantula went on.

"Worldwide, millions of people have watched that rescue and one of those people was Frankie Las Vegas. He loves you, Bob. He wants to make a film about you. It's going to be called *MOON MAN – A LUNAR ODYSSEY*! He's going to write it, direct it, produce it and star in it, and it's going to be shot entirely on the Moon. It's brilliant news, Bob. It's going to put us well and truly on the space map. We've arrived at last! Now… LET'S EAT CAKE!!"

Chapter Two

Over the years Bob had spent many a happy hour cavorting amongst the stars. However, most of those stars were burning balls of gas that hadn't featured in six mini-series, twelve motion pictures and an advert for Godfrey Whippet's Verucca Cream. Frankie Las Vegas, on the other hand, was a star who had shone in all those productions and now there he was in *Clapperboard Quarterly* discussing his next big blockbuster role... as THE MAN ON THE MOON!!

Reading the magazine as he blasted moonwards on the first day of filming, Bob was astonished to discover that so many people were involved in the making of a film. It was clear that in his job as 'special consultant' there would be a great deal of special consulting to do.

"I'll have to show the props person the exact kind of dusters Frankie should use in the cleaning scenes," thought Bob. "And I must warn the location lady not to film near the stubborn tea stains by Crater 573. Oh, and obviously I'll have to give the script a good going over – just to check Frankie's lunar lingo sounds right and that his 'Barry's woofs' are all in the right places."

As 'special consultant' Bob was expecting lots of questions from the cast and crew. So, as well as crafting himself a snazzy badge that read 'I'm Bob – stop me for help!!', he'd also had printed three hundred business cards to hand out to those in need.

And for Frankie Las Vegas, who Bob thought would need the most moon-man coaching, he had lovingly compiled a special

Bob, the Man on the Moon

Adviser to the stars
Purveyor of Moon wisdom

*Call me any time,
EVEN ON BINGO NIGHT!*

For Lunar helpline and intergalactic
telephone codes see reverse.

250-page *HANDBOOK OF HELPFUL HINTS*. It included 52 illustrations (23 in colour) and was broken down into easy-to-understand chapters such as:

1. VACUUMING TECHNIQUES
2. SOUVENIR TABLE ARRANGING
3. HOW TO LET TOURISTS DOWN GENTLY ABOUT THE NON-EXISTENCE OF ALIENS!!

"This could be the difference between Mr Las Vegas winning one of those glitzy awards or not!" said Bob.

But Barry wasn't listening. He'd been distracted by something outside the rocket porthole. Immediately Bob investigated and couldn't believe what he saw. Straight ahead, something was growing upwards directly from the Moon's surface.

"It looks like some kind of… HUGE HEAD!!" Bob gasped.

He was right. And, what's more, the head was getting bigger and bigger by the second. Then, as it continued to rise, a pair of shoulders appeared, followed by a body, arms and legs. It was incredible… It was awesome… IT WAS FRANKIE LAS VEGAS!! Or at least, on closer inspection, it was a MASSIVE, INFLATABLE REPLICA OF FRANKIE LAS VEGAS!

All around the Inflatable Frankie press rockets looped the loop, their camera flashes lighting up the darkness of space.

"WOW!" cried Bob. "It must be to mark the first day of filming."

Then suddenly, the Inflatable Frankie spoke.

"GREETINGS!" it said gruffly. "MY NAME IS BOB. YOU MIGHT KNOW ME BETTER AS THE MAN ON THE MOON. RIGHT NOW I'M ENJOYING A WELL-EARNED COFFEE BREAK BUT SOON I'LL BE ROCKETING TO DO BATTLE IN A CINEMA NEAR YOU!!! BE THERE! BECAUSE IF YOU'RE NOT WITH ME… YOU'RE WITH THEM!"

It was all most impressive but Bob was a little confused. "What kind of 'battle' is he talking about?" he asked Barry. "And who's the 'THEM'?" But as Barry was a dog, he couldn't provide any answers.

"What's muddling me more," continued Bob, "is that if that inflatable is meant to be Frankie playing me then where is his tank top? And why isn't his hair red? And why is he wearing denim jeans instead of sensible trousers and WHY, OH WHY IS HE ENJOYING A COFFEE BREAK INSTEAD OF A LOVELY TEA BREAK?? IT'S ALL WRONG!!"

Bob's brain was buzzing. Thank Jupiter they were nearly at the Moon.

"It seems Frankie's going to need this handbook more than I thought," said Bob. "A LOT MORE!!!"

Chapter Three

"Well, Barry," said Bob, on landing. "Without blowing my own trumpet it's obvious we are pretty blooming important to this film. I bet there's a VIP. stretch lunar limo on its way to pick us up – it'll probably have a big-screen TV and a fizzy-pop fridge."

Oddly, however, no VIP limo arrived. They were instead 'greeted' by a very angry rocket park attendant.

"OI!" he bellowed. "YOU CAN'T PARK THERE! THERE IS RESERVED FOR STARS AND BIGWIGS! ARE YOU A STAR?!"

"Well, not really," admitted Bob.

"Are you a bigwig then?"

"No. I'm Bob. You might know me better as the Man on the Moon."

The attendant was unimpressed. "I don't care if you're the Easter Bunny," he boomed. "If you're not on my stars and bigwigs list then you're not parking here. NOW MOVE IT – PRONTO!!"

So, having parked in the outer-crater rocket park, Bob and Barry made the long trek to the film set entrance. There, the welcome was equally cool. Two burly security guards in sunglasses barked out rule after rule, the most important of which seemed to be: "DO NOT BREAK WIND WITHIN FIFTY FEET OF MR LAS VEGAS!!"

"I can only promise to try," said Bob. Barry kept quiet.

Inside at last, Bob surveyed the lunar landscape.

The set reminded him of a documentary he'd once seen about anthills. Everywhere, people busied themselves like worker ants, moving cameras, lights, microphones, costumes and props. But where was Frankie? Bob needed to find him – sharpish. Without Bob's helpful handbook, Frankie would surely NEVER be able to do a convincing job of being Bob! The busy crew, however, were totally tight-lipped.

"But I'm Bob," he said. "You might know me better as the Man on the Moon. I'm a special consultant. Frankie needs me!"

Unfortunately no one seemed to care. Hardly anybody took one of Bob's business cards. And try as he might to be of help, he just seemed to be in the way.

"Well, I didn't know those two ruffians were actually stunt men rehearsing – it looked like they were having a right to-do," Bob muttered to Barry.

"And," he continued, "how could I have guessed that the black sticky tape cross by Crater 436 was showing Frankie where to stand for his scene? I was only trying to keep things tidy by peeling it off."

However, Bob WAS sure of one thing: NEW MOON CRATERS SHOULD ONLY EVER BE CREATED BY CRASHING ASTEROIDS –

NOT BY A BALDY STAGEHAND WITH A JACKHAMMER – which was what was happening in Lunar Zone 12. Bob shuddered. He was a more than a little cheesed off.

"I MUST STRONGLY PROTEST!" he declared. "HUMANS SHOULD NEVER MESS WITH THE LUNAR CRATER QUOTA – NOT EVEN FOR A SUPER FILM SCENE!"

The stagehand ignored him and so, as politely as possible, Bob pounced. With the help of Barry's snapping and woofing, he grabbed the juddering jackhammer away from the startled fellow. But the jackhammer was too strong for Bob – his arms just weren't muscly enough to control it, and, with a life of its own, it vibrated across the set, cutting through cables, knocking over floodlights and generally leaving carnage in its wake. It was chaos.

Now it was the security guards in sunglasses who were terribly cheesed off. Rolling up their sleeves, they launched their attack.

"S S C A A A A R R R P E E R R ! !" shouted Bob to Barry. And scarper they did, straight into a clothes rail of costumes.

That little mistake proved to be disasterous. Temporarily blinded by a pea-green alien head, Bob staggered, tripped and slipped until, with a crash and a smash, he stumbled and tumbled deep, deep down – into Crater 368.

Luckily his bottom met with a soft landing. Unluckily that soft landing was Frankie Las Vegas himself!

Chapter Four

Bob, the Man on the Moon, was worried. Never before in the history of the universe had he been summoned to Infinity House… on a Thursday.

"Hmm…" he said, shooting upwards in the lift, "we probably can't blame it on the nuns this time, Barry."

Waiting outside the office, Bob could hear Tarantula on the phone. "Yes, Mr Las Vegas. No, Mr Las Vegas. You're the boss, Mr Las Vegas."

Bob's unfortunate crater tumble had wrecked a very important scene. When Frankie Las Vegas had shouted "ACTION!" he'd got much more action than he'd bargained for. By the time he'd wheezed "CUT" he was lying spread-eagled on the crater floor with a bruised everything and a red-haired astronaut sitting on his chest. Around him lay smashed lights and cameras. Underneath him were the remains of his treasured director's chair. It couldn't have got any worse. But then Bob broke wind and it did.

Inside his office Tarantula's moustache was droopy again. Even a cake with 'SORRY' written on it in edible gold leaf couldn't improve his mood. Doodling skulls on his notepad, Tarantula didn't look up as he spoke.

"Dick, the Man on Titus 10, has come a cropper on holiday," he said sharply. "You are to fill in for him on Titus 10 immediately and indefinitely. GOOD DAY!"

"But what about the filming?" Bob asked. "They need me. I'm THEIR INSPIRATION!!"

Still Tarantula didn't look up. "I BELIEVE I SAID GOOD DAY!" he repeated.

Bob had no choice. With a heavy heart, he turned to go.

"I warned Dick not to go bungee jumping over Crocodile Creek," he sighed.

***

The Titus 10 moon was a stone's throw from the edge of the universe. Everyday, as an astro professional Bob gave his all. He cleaned and hoovered and polished... but he couldn't help thinking of his own beloved Moon, and Frankie Las Vegas's film. What had the inflatable Frankie-Bob been talking about? Why was Tarantula calling Frankie "boss"? And when would someone, ANYONE, call the special lunar helpline number on his business cards?

He reassured himself with the fact that he'd left a copy of his handbook with one of the burly security guards. "Whether I'm there or not, that will tell them all they need to know," he said. "They'll do a grand job. I completely trust them!"

But then, one dreary Thursday, as Bob dozed on the long journey home, something on Space FM woke him with a start.

"And tonight," said DJ Drivel, "the great and the good of showbiz are out in force on the Moon for the red-carpet premiere of *MOON MAN – A LUNAR ODYSSEY*. A state-of-the-art outdoor cinema has been specially constructed for the invited stars and bigwigs to enjoy the first showing of this all-action lunar adventure!"

Bob was stunned. "STARS ALIVE, BARRY!" he gasped. "OUR INVITE MUST HAVE BEEN LOST IN THE POST!!!!"

There wasn't a moment to waste. Pulling the sharpest of U-turns, Bob zoomed towards his beloved Moon. From a distance he could see the beams of two brilliant strobe lights dancing amongst the stars. And then, sure enough, there it was – the spectacular cinema, the celebrities in penguin suits and gowns, dripping in jewellery, and on the big screen, as tall as a skyscraper: *MOON MAN – A LUNAR ODYSSEY.*

At least Bob *thought* it was the Moon Man movie. Frankie Las Vegas didn't look a bit like Bob. His hair was still dark and his suit was GOLD! He was wearing a necklace and even had a TATTOO. And worst of all, his badge was black and white striped instead of Bob's favourite red and white! It was a CATASTROPHE!

"NO, NO, NO!!!" he exclaimed. "IT'S ALL WRONG!!! AND LOOK AT THAT MINI VACUUM CLEANER HE'S HOLDING – THAT WOULD BE NO MATCH FOR MOON DUST!!"

Worse, Bob soon realised that in fact it wasn't a vacuum cleaner that Frankie Bob was holding at all. IT WAS A LASER RAYGUN 2000. AND HE WASN'T TRYING TO COMBAT MOON DUST! HE WAS TRYING TO COMBAT… ALIENS!!

Slowly, Bob slumped back in his pilot seat. "Oh dear, oh dear, oh dear," he sighed.

Chapter Five

"MY NAME IS BOB!" bellowed Frankie-Bob. "YOU MIGHT KNOW ME BETTER AS YOUR WORST NIGHTMARE! THE MOON IS MINE – ALL MINE – AND I'D DESTROY EVERY LAST INCH OF IT BEFORE I'D LET ANY SNIVELLING GREEN PIECES OF SLIME FROM DEEP SPACE TRASHVILLE GET THEIR GRUBBY MITTS ON IT!!"

Certainly he seemed true to his word. With an arsenal of laser guns, flame-throwers and missile launchers, Frankie-Bob threw himself into all-out war against the King of Aliens and his pea-green centurions.

KABOOOM! went the explosions.
KAPOW!! went the laser fights.

As his rocket circled the cinema Bob was close to tears.

"He's not me to a tee at all!" he whimpered.

Admittedly Bob had missed the beginning of the film but he was pretty sure that it hadn't opened with the rousing vacuuming scenes he'd been expecting. In fact, Frankie-Bob didn't look as though he would EVER do any cleaning. And, amidst all the fighting to the death, when on earth would he find time to organise his souvenir table or rehearse his Moon-themed variety show?

"AND HOW MANY TIMES DO I HAVE TO TELL PEOPLE? ALIENS DO NOT EXIST!!" Bob cried.

Bob flew his rocket faster and faster, circling the cinema. In an attempt to distract the audience he performed spectacular zigzags and loop-the-loops. But no one noticed him. He had no choice but to use the rocket's loudspeaker:

"STARS AND BIGWIGS!!" he shouted. "AVERT YOUR EYES FROM THE SCREEN! THIS FILM IS A LIE! ALIENS DO NOT EXIST! I REPEAT: ALIENS DO NOT EXIST! PLEASE ABANDON THIS PREMIERE AT ONCE!!"

But everybody was still engrossed in the action. What could possibly be so interesting about Frankie-Bob? Couldn't they see he was nothing but a gun-slinging nincompoop who didn't care for the Moon at all? In fact, he was beginning to get up Bob's nose.

"RIGHT, THAT'S IT!" Bob said. "I THINK IT'S ABOUT TIME I GOT UP *HIS* NOSE!!"

On the screen was the latest of many Frankie-Bob close-ups.

"COME AND GET IT!" Frankie hollered at the King of Aliens. "DESTRUCTION IS SERVED!!" Then he laughed a terrible laugh that echoed throughout the cosmos. Flaring wildly, his giant-sized nostrils were like a red rag to a Bob.

"WHAT I DO NOW," declared Bob, "I DO IN THE GOOD NAME OF THE MAN ON THE MOON!!" Then he directed his rocket towards Frankie-Bob's enormous face.

"HOLD ON TIGHT, BARRY!" he shouted.

"WE'RE GOING IN!!"

And with an almighty RRRIIIIIPP!!! Bob's rocket bulleted through the screen right up the actor's nose. With skilful manoeuvring, Bob navigated his rocket back and forth, in and out of the giant screen, through Frankie's ears and mouth. Within seconds, the screen was peppered with holes. The premiere was over.

Bob was about to embark on stage two of his plan, *Win over the audience with lunar logic*, but, as he opened his hatch, he was greeted by a chorus of boos. Crowded around Bob's rocket was an army of grumpy celebrities led by none other than Frankie Las Vegas himself.

"Good evening Mr Las Vegas," Bob said politely. "My name is Bob. You might know me better as…"

"…THE EX-ASTRONAUT," interrupted Frankie angrily, "WHO, AFTER TONIGHT, WILL NEVER SET FOOT ON THE MOON AGAIN!!"

Chapter Six

As he sat on the steps of Infinity House waiting for Tarantula Van Trumpet, Bob pondered his problem. All night, the smug face of Frankie Las Vegas had been smirking down at him from the poster for:

MOON MAN
A LUNAR ODYSSEY

that adorned the wall of the Puddle Lane Picture House. And all night the words from Frankie's speech had rung in his ears:

"THIS VERY AFTERNOON I MADE AN OFFER TO BUY THIS MOON AND THAT OFFER WAS ACCEPTED. NOW I'M IN

CHARGE, SO LET ME BE CLEAR: YOU, BOB, ARE NO LONGER WELCOME HERE! THE MOON IS MINE – ALL MINE. AND I WOULD DESTROY EVERY LAST INCH OF IT BEFORE I'D LET A LITTLE GOODY TWO-SHOES FROM HOME-MADE HANDBOOKS STUPIDVILLE GET HIS GRUBBY MITTS ON IT! GUARDS! EJECT THIS TRESPASSER AT ONCE!!"

Unfortunately, Bob was fairly certain that the contents of his piggy bank (seven pounds, sixty-three pence, two buttons and a football sticker) would not be enough to buy back the Moon, even if the sticker was of Brazilian superstar, Socrates Clump.

At 8.30 a.m. Tarantula finally turned up on his motorised scooter. He didn't look surprised to see Bob.

"You'd better come up," he said.

Back in his office Tarantula sat down and

immediately began to doodle skulls on his
notepad. He didn't look up as he spoke.

"Frankie went above my head, Bob," he
said, "to the big bosses. I tried to stop them
selling but I couldn't. Frankie was offering too
much money. And when he promised them a
share of the profits of his new Moon Man
venture, that sealed the deal."

Bob was confused.

"Moon Man venture?" he said. "What
Moon Man venture?"

Tarantula sighed and pointed to the window. "Look out there, Bob," he said. "Frankie Las Vegas is a superstar."

Opposite, Bob could see the queue outside the Puddle Lane Picture House was ten deep and snaked out of sight. The film-goers were singing and chanting like a football crowd. "MOON MAN! MOON MAN! MOON MAN!"

"Like it or lump it," continued Tarantula, "Frankie knew that *MOON MAN – A LUNAR ODYSSEY* was destined to become the most popular film of all time and he was always going to try to make as much money from it as possible."

"But the filming's over. Why does he still need the Moon?"

Tarantula sighed again as he reached into his desk drawer and pulled out a piece of paper.

"This advert," he said, "will be published tomorrow in every newspaper in the entire galaxy."

Bob took the advert and read it:

He went pale.

"A theme park?" Bob cried. "MY MOON is going to become a tacky, rubbish-strewn THEME PARK!!? NO! NO! NO! WE CAN'T LET IT HAPPEN! WE'VE GOT TO DO SOMETHING!!"

"It's too late!" said Tarantula. "I've tried everything. From today I am permanently assigning you to Titus 10 and there's nothing more to say on the matter. I'm sorry Bob."

But Bob had a LOT more to say.

"I'm sorry, Mr Trumpet," he said bravely, "but I don't want to work on Titus 10. I am the Man on the Moon – the EARTH'S Moon – and if I can't do that then… then I DON'T WANT TO BE AN ASTRONAUT AT ALL." Bob could hardly believe the words that were coming out of his very own mouth.

"MR TRUMPET," he shouted, "I QUIT!!"

Chapter Seven

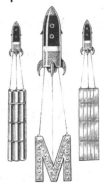

That evening, as the heavens opened, Bob could hear cargo rockets zooming Moonwards with steel, glass, wood and plastic. Soon the peaceful serenity of the Moon would be replaced by the all-action, block-busting rides, shops and restaurants of Frankie Las Vegas's theme park.

"Rome wasn't built in a day," he'd boasted earlier on TV, "but Moon Man Land will be. SO BE HERE TOMORROW NIGHT, BECAUSE IF YOU'RE NOT WITH ME... YOU'RE WITH THEM!!"

In just one day, almost everyone in the world had seen the film and loved it. Cinemas were showing it around the clock. Big screens had been projecting it in football stadiums, parks, jungles, across deserts and on top of mountains. There had even been a special underwater matinee for deep-sea divers and submariners.

To Bob's dismay Frankie was now seen as some kind of hero figure. Even the American president had been spotted jogging in the grounds of the White House in a T-shirt reading 'BACK OFF ALIENS! I'M WITH BOB!'

"He's not fit to polish a real astronaut's space boots!" he'd snapped, turning off the TV.

Outside, the rain was getting heavier. As Bob gazed out on to the gloomy street, he could see the reflection of the Moon shivering and quivering in a tear-shaped puddle… as if it was crying for help. And that's when sixteen important words suddenly popped up out of Bob's memory.

"I HEREBY PROMISE, FOR BETTER OR WORSE, TO ALWAYS PUT THE GOOD OF THE MOON FIRST."

It was the oath Bob had taken on his astro-graduation day. There and then, Bob hatched a plan. It would need a cunning disguise and a bucket full of bravery, not least during their visit to BARNETTA WIGGINS' CUTTING SHACK!

Three hours later Bob and Barry emerged transformed by two dramatic changes of image.

"Those two burly security guards will

never recognise us now, Barry," cried Bob. "And when we get inside Moon Man Land, we will deal with this mess once and for all. We'd better get a wriggle on though. The tourists' rockets will be jetting off soon. It's time for us to go and SAVE OUR MOON!!!"

Chapter Eight

Bob could feel the beads of sweat welling on his brow as he queued in front of the giant entrance to Moon Man Land. Around him, excited tourists dressed as Frankie-Bob finger-zapped other tourists dressed as aliens. Some quoted lines from the film. Others happily hummed the theme tune. Up ahead, the two burly, mean-looking security guards were checking tickets. Above them was a poster of Bob and Barry. It read:

This man and his dog are MOON MENACES and could INVADE AT ANY TIME TO DESTROY YOUR FUN.

SHOULD YOU SEE THEM SHOUT "INVASION!" AND THEY WILL BE IMMEDIATELY TERMINATED!

Bob gulped.

Never had so much rested on the curls of

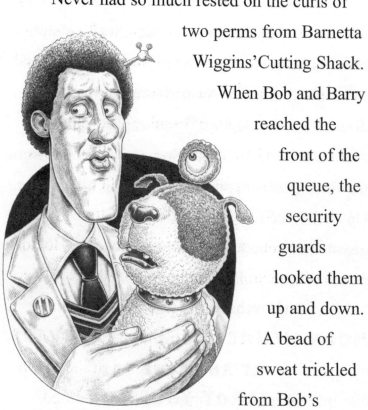

two perms from Barnetta Wiggins'Cutting Shack. When Bob and Barry reached the front of the queue, the security guards looked them up and down. A bead of sweat trickled from Bob's

forehead and quivered on the edge of his nose.
For a second, the universe held its breath… until
the two security guards nodded in tandem.

"In you go," they said.

They'd done it! Without looking back, Bob
and Barry scuttled through the gates.

Moon Man Land was vast and ugly. Every
last inch had been covered with a thick plastic
flooring from which sprouted Moon Man themed
rides, rollercoasters and amusement arcades, all
plastered with images of Frankie-Bob zapping
aliens. Everywhere there were stalls and kiosks
selling expensive plastic rubbish. The smell of
greasy burgers lingered in Bob's nostrils and the
Moon Man soundtrack assaulted his ears. Hoards
of workers wearing huge Frankie-Bob heads were
handing out vouchers for fizzy pops and chips.
No one was offered a single lunar fact, stat or
nugget of history. The real meaning of the Moon
didn't seem to matter anymore. No one cared.

"OK, Barry," said Bob, "let's act normal, get to know the park, find its weaknesses, then we'll strike."

And so they began a frenetic day of riding, queing, eating and spending. It ended with Bob and Barry strapped into the stomach-churning ALIEN DOOMSDAY DESTRUCTION RIDE!

For what seemed like a lifetime Bob and Barry were launched and plunged, up and down, round and round. Finally, they ploughed at one hundred miles an hour through a raging channel of water, soaking everybody on board. As they shakily stepped off, sodden and wet, a little boy in a Frankie-Bob Moon Man T-shirt turned to stare at Barry.

"IT'S THE DOG FROM THE POSTER!" he shouted. "I N V A A A A S S I O O N!!" Immediately all eyes were on Barry. Bob looked down and gulped. BARRY'S PERM HAD FALLEN OUT! THE WATER HAD TOTALLY STRAIGHTENED HIS FUR! HE LOOKED LIKE THE OLD BARRY AGAIN!!

The security guards' eyes moved from Barry to Bob. They knew that wherever Barry was, Bob would be too.

"WE'VE BEEN RUMBLED!!" cried Bob. "S C A A A R R P P E E R R!!"

Bob and Barry pelted across Moon Man Land, snaking in and out of rides, burger vans and crowds of people. But they couldn't shake the ticked-off security guards.

Making a U-turn past the Cosmic Kebab station, they found themselves in front of countless rows of Portaloos.

"Look Barry, outside Portaloo 672," cried Bob. "It's one of those large costume heads belonging to a Frankie-Bob character. Its owner must be spending a penny – quick, it's the perfect getaway disguise."

Tucking Barry inside his coat, Bob swiftly put on the head, poking his arms out of the holes in the side. They were just in the nick of time. Seconds later, the security guards galloped past. It was as if Bob and Barry had disappeared.

"Phew, that was a close shave!" said Bob. "Perhaps we'd better keep ourselves hidden away in here, just until the coast is clear."

Bob's whispers seemed to echo through their hiding place. It crossed his mind that this great, big, hollow head was probably very much like Frankie's real great, big, hollow head. But there was one crucial difference. The real Frankie's head would NEVER have given up its important secrets to Bob. But this one did!

Chapter Nine

It was late by the time Bob and Barry managed to leave Moon Man Land, but back home there was no time for sleep. While it was still fresh in his mind, Bob was quickly writing the secrets of the head down onto his notepad. Written on the head's inside surface had been maps, diagrams, price lists and key codes, all for the benefit of Moon Man Land employees. But it was the EVENT SCHEDULE that Bob was most interested in.

FRIDAY 13TH, Bob had learnt, would be INVASION DAY!! When Frankie Las Vegas would make a surprise special appearance at Moon Man Land. Firstly he was to star in a live re-enactment of the Moon Man film complete with his laser-zapping licking of the King of Aliens and his pea-green centurions. But it was the aftershow plans that had chilled Bob to the bone. After his performance, Frankie would announce that, by the end of the month, every moon in the universe would become its own Moon Man Land.

"HOLY HELMETS!!" Bob gasped. "WE CAN'T LET THAT HAPPEN!! EVER!!!"

Immediately, Bob got to work. The information was studied. Letters were written. Help was requested and a plan was hatched.

"IF IT'S INVASION DAY THEY WANT," Bob declared, "THEN IT'S INVASION DAY THEY SHALL HAVE!!"

By the time Friday 13th arrived everything was in place. The plan HAD to work. Bob could see from Earth that, after only a few days, the Moon had dulled in the sky. It looked tired and lifeless, as if it couldn't breathe.

On the Moon itself, the happy atmosphere had quickly disappeared. Long queues for rollercoasters, fast food and souvenirs were making people cross. Rides kept breaking down and the prices kept going up. Still though, like hypnotised robots, the people came and each day they cared a little less about the Moon they once had loved.

At precisely ten o'clock the crowds were ushered towards the performance arena. On stage, a mist had descended and eerie music filled the air. Suddenly, with an almighty crashing of cymbals and flashing of lights, the stage was flooded by a thousand peeved pea-green centurions. The re-enactment of the Moon Man movie had begun!

The audience was captivated. Open-mouthed, they "OOOHED" and "AAAHED" as before their very eyes, emerging through the haze, came the gun-blasting Frankie-Bob himself. With a KABOOOM and a KAPOOOW and a CABOOOSH he felled one alien after another. The crowd cheered their appreciation.

"BLAST THEM TO SMITHEREENS!!" screamed Pippy Chuckles.

"SHOW NO MERCY!!" screeched Gideon Humberdunk.

Frankie-Bob happily granted their requests and soon, against the battered smoking backdrop, not a single alien was left standing. Once again, the eerie music descended upon the stage.

"KING OF ALIENS!" shouted Frankie-Bob. "REVEAL YOURSELF AND PREPARE FOR YOUR DOOM!"

Right on cue, a faint droning sound could be heard. It seemed to be coming from above and it was getting louder. The crowd craned their necks to look out into space, and noticed a speck advancing quickly towards the Moon. The speck grew bigger and bigger until they could make out, through squinted eyes, arms, legs and a head wild with rage. The people gasped. They loved it.

Never before had they witnessed such a spectacular special effect. Excitedly, Chesterton Beetroot turned his gaze back to the stage.

"IT'S THE KING OF ALIENS!!!" he roared. "HE'S COMING, BOB! KICK HIS BOTTOM!!"

But Frankie-Bob was in no fit state to kick anyone's bottom. For right there, in front of everybody, the jaw-droppingly handsome, all-conquering saviour of the cosmos was frozen to the spot and crying like an iddy, biddy baby.

Chapter Ten

The people in the audience looked at each other in confusion. Frankie Las Vegas hadn't shown any fear in the Moon Man film. He hadn't whimpered or blubbered. He was never frozen by fear. And nobody could remember a scene where every pea-green centurion sprang back to life and ran away screaming from their very own king.

And then the penny dropped.

"I'VE A FEELING THAT ISN'T ACTUALLY THE KING OF ALIENS!!" screamed Foggarty Dewdrop.

"IT M… MUST BE A REAL ALIEN INVASION!!" shrieked Percival Dingdong.

"R U U U U U U U N N N N N !!!"

A panic-fuelled mad scramble to escape the Moon followed. Rockets had to swerve to avoid hitting each other. Some clipped the top of the ALIEN DOOMSDAY DESTRUCTION ride causing it to teeter and collapse directly on to the Portaloos, their scattered contents adding extra strength to the stench of fear. Soon all that was left behind was a trampled Moon of half-eaten hot dogs, broken rides and abandoned Frankie-Bob heads.

From the safety of Earth, the people looked up at their moon in horror. It didn't shimmer. It didn't glimmer. Moon Man Land had poisoned the whole surface of the Moon, making it look weak and defenceless. And so, when the fiery alien disappeared around the far side of the Moon, they tearfully feared the worst. Certainly Frankie-Bob had proved to be far too wimpy to save it.

With trembling voices, news reporters around the world reported on the images beaming down from Moon Man Land cameras. In the middle of the dust cloud created by thousands of blast-offs, Frankie was now alone, still paralysed with fear, expecting the terrifying alien invader to appear on the lunar horizon at any moment.

However, what ACTUALLY emerged through the dust was a red-quiffed astronaut with his unusual dog. For once, Frankie was delighted to see them.

"BOB! THANK G-GOODNESS!!" he squealed. "YOU'VE GOT TO S-SAVE ME! THERE'S A HUGE A-ACTOR-EATING ALIEN ON ITS WAY! I BEG YOU TO SAVE M-ME!!"

Bob was unmoved. Instead, he dramatically thrust his arms, fists clenched, above his head and, accompanied by a chorus of Barry's howls, shouted out:

"ALIEN INVADER!! COME FORTH!! REVEAL YOURSELF!! LET THE INVASION BEGIN!!!"

Right on cue, the massive, scaley alien roared up over the horizon and strode towards them. On Earth, the people were glued to their screens.

"PLEASE DON'T LET IT GET ME, BOB!!" sobbed Frankie-Bob. "I'M SORRY FOR

EVERYTHING! I'LL DO ANYTHING!!"

"Anything?!" asked Bob.

"ANYTHING!!" confirmed Frankie.

"THEN SELL ME BACK THE MOON! I'LL GIVE YOU SEVEN POUNDS, SIXTY-THREE PENCE, TWO BUTTONS AND A FOOTBALL STICKER OF SOCRATES CLUMP!! Is it a deal?!"

The raging alien was approaching fast.

"YES, YES!" bawled Frankie. "IT'S A DEAL! NOW FOR PITY'S SAKE, CALL OFF THAT ALIEN!!"

"Alien?" said Bob calmly. "But Frankie, there are no such things as aliens."

And, with those words he sharply clapped his hands and something incredible happened. All of a sudden, the alien invader COMPLETELY BROKE APART.

Frankie couldn't believe his red raw eyes. Neither could those watching on Earth.

"WHAT THE DICKENS IS GOING ON?" gasped TV presenter Puddleton Wick.

"Quick, let's go to the action-replay," urged his celebrity guest, Stella Prunella Smythe.

A slow-motion replay would reveal all. Everyone on Earth was astonished: the King of the Aliens was neither a king nor an alien. He was an illusion, made up of all the rockets and spaceships belonging to every Moon Man in the cosmos. Spray-painted green and skilfully flying in carefully rehearsed formations, they created the giant frame of a fearsome giant. Its mighty roar was the combined roars of all the engines and the fire in its nostrils had been space distress flares.

And now, as the rockets broke ranks and landed, the alien had dissolved and the real invasion could begin. One by one, the Moon Men disembarked, not with laser guns but with vacuum cleaners, dusters and bin bags, and the clean-up began.

As the cameras panned around, the watching crowds back on Earth saw what a sorry state the Moon had come to under the ownership of Frankie Las Vegas.

"I can't believe we trusted an actor."

"He was a total fraud."

"And he didn't take care of our moon."

"Shame on him and on us."

"Thank Jupiter for Bob – he saved the Moon!" cried Mildred Ball.

"YES – HE'S THE REAL HERO!" added Roberto Salmon.

With Bob's clean-up operation in full swing, on Earth, the Moon was becoming brighter by the minute. Happy moonbeams lit up the shining smiles of the people. Never again would the people of Earth forget to love and take care of their Moon.

Later, as Bob saluted his departing Moon Man friends, they responded by flying their rockets into a beautiful Bob-shaped formation. The Lunar War was over.

"That's a wrap, Barry!" said Bob. "From now on, the only stars for us are the ones twinkling above our heads."

And with that, they settled down for a lovely cup of tea and a juicy bone.

THE DOWN-AND-OU

ALA

Playing i
Decemb

LAYERS PRESENT

ODIN

STARRING
FORMER FILM STAR

FRANKIE LAS VEGAS

AS

THE WIDOW TWANKIE!

rington by the sea
st to January 28th

TEMPLAR PUBLISHING presents
a SIMON BARTRAM production
a BOB AND BARRY film

BOB'S FILM FIASCO

Starring
Bob, Man on the Moon and
his best-ever friend Barry

Supporting Cast
Tarantula Van Trumpet
Frankie Las Vegas
DJ Drivel
Barnetta Wiggins
Puddleton Wink
Stella Prunella Smythe
Mildred Ball
Roberto Salmon

Writer: Simon Bartram
Editor: Libby Hamilton
Production Designer: Will Steele
Casting Director: Alison Eldred
Producer: Helen Boyle
Director: Amanda Wood

Young Harry Hammer would give his right fin to be as fast as a blue shark, as cool as a tiger shark, or as downright terrifying as a great white.

Determined to prove that he's just as brave, tough and scary as any fish in the sea, Harry throws himself into a series of daring adventures, in which only his loyal friends – and his own unique hammerhead abilities – keep him out of trouble.

May 2013
ISBN: 978-1-84877-732-3

May 2013
ISBN: 978-1-84877-733-0

May 2013
ISBN: 978-1-84877-734-7

May 2013
ISBN: 978-1-84877-735-4

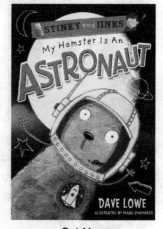